Ann of Green Gables

Written by Lucy Maud Montgomery

Retold by Sarah Webb

Illustrated by Jim Mitchell

Collins

Anne arrives in Avonlea

As soon as she stepped off the steam train on that spring day, Anne knew there was something special about Avonlea. The scent of apple blossom filled the air and there were horses playing in the field behind the station, under a wild cherry tree. After the noise and dirt of the city, Prince Edward Island seemed like heaven.

So far, Anne hadn't had much luck with her foster families – the last one had sent her back to the orphanage – but maybe the small town of Avonlea would be different. She certainly hoped so. All she'd ever wanted was a home with a family who loved her.

Anne stood still and looked around the small station. The other Avonlea passengers had left; she was alone. Mrs Spencer, who'd travelled with her from the orphanage, had told her to wait on the platform for her new family, the Cuthberts, to collect her, but there was no sign of them. Sighing, she swung her old carpet bag over her shoulder, walked towards the green wooden bench and sat down. She waited, and waited and waited.

She was just about to give up hope when she spotted a horse and carriage throwing up dust on the road. As it came closer, Anne could see a tall, older man in a dark suit driving. Could it be Mr Cuthbert?

Abandoning her carpet bag, Anne ran towards him, waving frantically. "Mr Cuthbert?" she called. "Are you Mr Cuthbert of Green Gables?"

The man pulled up the carriage and stared down at her. "I am," he said slowly. "And who are you?"

"Anne Shirley, of course. Your orphan." She smoothed down the front of her yellow cotton dress and straightened her thick red plaits.

Mr Cuthbert looked confused. He stroked his grey beard. "Our orphan? But you're – " he stopped mid-sentence. "Never mind."

She gave him a warm smile. "I was starting to worry that you weren't coming for me. I was imagining what I'd do if you didn't arrive. I figured I'd climb that cherry tree over in the field with the horses and sleep there all night. That'd be a magical place to sleep, don't you think?"

Now he looked even more confused. "I don't really know," he said. After a long pause, he added, "I'm sorry I was late. Let's get going. We've a fair way to travel to Green Gables, and my sister will be worrying about us."

Anne sat beside Mr Cuthbert in the carriage and chatted away to him as they drove up the steep hill and along a road fringed with more wild cherry trees.

"What does that pink blossom remind you of?" she asked him.

"I don't really know," he replied, feeling a little bewildered. He'd never been asked such a question before.

"It reminds me of a party dress," she said, sighing dreamily. "I've never had my own party dress. But I've imagined all kinds of beautiful dresses, all silk and satin. I love using my imagination, don't you?" She smiled at him. "Don't tell me. You don't really know."

"That's right," he said, sounding amused rather than cross. "How did you guess?" He smiled back at her, his grey eyes kind.

7

He smiled again when she renamed the main avenue in Avonlea "The White Way of Delight", and his neighbours' pond "The Lake of Shining Waters".

By the time they reached Green Gables, it was dark outside. Feeling stiff and tired, Anne climbed down from the carriage and followed Mr Cuthbert towards the porch of a large wooden farmhouse.

Mr Cuthbert opened the front door. There was a lamp lit in the hall and a woman in a plain blue dress rushed towards them. She looked at Anne suspiciously and then back at her brother. She folded her arms across her chest, tilted her chin up and demanded, "Who on earth is this, Matthew? And where's our boy?"

The mistake

"This is our orphan, Marilla," Matthew said. He was shifting from foot to foot and he looked very uncomfortable.

"There must be some mistake," Marilla said, frowning. "What was Mrs Spencer thinking? The message I sent was to fetch me a boy from the orphanage to help with the farm."

"I couldn't just leave her alone at the station," Matthew said.

Marilla shook her head. "She'll have to go back."

"You don't want me?" Anne wailed. "I should've known it was all too good to last. Oh, this is the most tragical thing that's ever happened to me!" And with that she burst into tears.

The edges of Marilla's mouth twitched. "You can stay here until we work out what to do with you. What's your name?"

"Will you please call me Cordelia?" Anne begged. Marilla frowned. "Is that your name?"

"No, but isn't Cordelia an elegant name? My name is Anne Shirley. If you must call me Anne, can you call me Anne spelt with an 'e'? It looks so much nicer. If you'll call me Anne with an 'e', I won't mind so much not being called Cordelia."

Marilla gave in. "Very well then, Anne with 'e' it is. Now I'll show you to your room." She led Anne up the wooden stairs and into a small, plain room. It had whitewashed walls, a bare wooden floor with a circular rag rug and an old-fashioned bed.

Anne changed into her old nightdress and jumped under the covers, pulling them over her head.

"Good night," she heard Marilla say.

Anne popped her head out again to wail. "How can you call it a good night? It's the worst night I've ever had in my life." Then she dived under her covers again. As soon as she heard Marilla close the door behind her, Anne felt terrible. She wanted to stay at Green Gables so much, she cried herself to sleep.

The next morning, on the carriage ride over to Mrs Spencer's house to sort out the mistake, Marilla said, "It's a long enough drive and I was thinking last night I don't know much about you, child. What age are you? And where are you from?"

"Eleven," Anne said. "I was born in Nova Scotia, Canada. My mother died of a fever when I was three months old and Father died four days later. A lady called Mrs Thomas took me in and then when she didn't want me any more, I lived with Mrs Hammond and her eight children. She had three sets of twins, can you imagine? I used to get so tired carrying them around. And then she went to America and I ended up in the orphanage. And then Mrs Spencer came to collect me."

"Were those women good to you?" Marilla asked thoughtfully.

Anne's face went red. "Oh, I'm sure they meant to be good and kind. But they weren't always."

Marilla was quiet until they reached Mrs Spencer's door. She explained the mistake about Anne to Mrs Spencer who said, "Really? Goodness I'm so sorry, Marilla. Now, there's no harm done as Mrs Blewett would like a girl to help with her children. She's right here, in fact. Mrs Blewett!" she called.

A woman with a sharp chin and beady eyes walked outside and stared at Anne. "You'll do," Mrs Blewett snapped.

"My baby never stops crying and I need a rest. I'll take you home right now."

Anne's face dropped. Another baby!

Marilla took in Anne's sad face and started to feel sorry for the girl. Marilla knew she wouldn't get much kindness at Mrs Blewett's house. "I don't think it's right that Anne should have to mind a baby when she's only a child herself," she told Mrs Blewett firmly. "Maybe having a girl around the house wouldn't be such a bad thing, after all."

"Oh, Marilla!" Anne gasped, beaming at her. "Thank you, thank you!"

"Don't get too excited, Anne," Marilla added. "I need to discuss it with Matthew first and we'll decide tomorrow."

That evening, Anne found it impossible to sleep. She lay in her bed thinking about what Marilla had said, and whispered to herself, "Please let me stay at Green Gables."

The trouble with Mrs Lynde

The following morning, Anne couldn't wait to hear Marilla and Matthew's decision. "Won't you tell me if you're going to send me away or not?" she begged. "Please, Marilla?"

"I've never brought up a child, especially a girl," Marilla said, "and I may make a terrible mess of it, but we've decided to keep you, Anne. So long as you can manage to be good and grateful. Now, why on earth are you crying?"

"I'm just so happy," Anne sobbed. "I promise I'll try to be good. Can I call you Aunt Marilla? I've never had an aunt."

Marilla's lips twitched with a smile. "No, because I'm not your aunt. Plain old Marilla will do."

***

That afternoon, their neighbour, Mrs Lynde, called in to meet Anne. "I've heard a lot about your new orphan girl already," she told Marilla.

"She's a bright little thing," Marilla said proudly. "She has her faults, but I must say the house seems different already. Even though I had my doubts, I do believe she's growing on me."

Mrs Lynde stared Anne up and down, when she bounded in cheerfully from the orchard. "Well, they didn't pick you for your looks, that's for sure," she said. "You're skinny and plain and I've never seen so many freckles on a girl's face. And your hair! It's the colour of carrots."

Anne's face flushed as red as her hair. "How dare you call me plain and freckly? You're a rude, unkind woman! I hate you!" Marilla was so shocked at Anne's outburst that she was speechless for a few seconds. How could she bring up such a wild girl? Then, not knowing what else to do, she snapped, "Anne! Go to your room and stay there."

19

Anne stamped up the stairs and slammed the door behind her, her eyes full of angry tears.

A few minutes later, Marilla walked into Anne's room and found her face down on the bed, her eyes red and swollen from crying.

"Anne?" Marilla said. "I know Mrs Lynde hurt your feelings, but you were very rude. You must apologise to her."

"Never!" Anne replied stubbornly. "You can punish me all you like, but I shan't say sorry."

"Then you'll stay in your room until you do."

A whole day passed and Anne still refused to apologise to Mrs Lynde. The following evening, a concerned Matthew tiptoed into her room. "Won't you apologise, Anne?" he pleaded. "It's too quiet downstairs without you."

Anne was very fond of Matthew and she missed talking to him, too. He was the sweetest, dearest man in the world. She didn't want him to think badly of her. She thought about it for a little while. Mrs Lynde had been unkind to her, but maybe it wouldn't be so awful to say sorry after all.

She smiled at Matthew. "For you, I will."

It was with much relief that Marilla walked Anne to Mrs Lynde's house. But on their arrival, to everyone's complete astonishment, Anne fell on her knees on Mrs Lynde's floor and held out her hands. "Oh, Mrs Lynde," she wailed. "I'm so sorry for being rude to you. I've made Marilla and Matthew sad and they've been so kind to me. You were only telling the truth: I am freckly and plain and I do have red hair. Please forgive me?"

"There, there, child," Mrs Lynde said, quickly warming to the girl who was kneeling so hopefully on her best rug. "Of course I forgive you. I'm sorry I hurt your feelings. And I think your hair is a beautiful colour, like autumn leaves."

Anne gave Mrs Lynde a big smile. "Thank you, Mrs Lynde. Can I please look around your garden before I go back to Green Gables? It's so beautiful."

Mrs Lynde was delighted. She was very proud of her garden. "Of course you can, Anne. And you may pick some of my white lilies for your bedroom."

On the way home, Anne held onto Marilla's hand and asked her, "Did you like my apology?"

Marilla's mouth twitched as if she was trying not to smile. "It was a good one all right," she replied. In fact, she'd enjoyed seeing Mrs Lynde change her mind about Anne almost as much as she enjoyed the feeling of Anne's hand in hers.

Anne meets her best friend

"How would you like to make a new friend?" Marilla asked Anne the following week. "I'm calling over to Mrs Barry's house this afternoon and she has a daughter your age called Diana."

Anne gasped. "Oh, Marilla, I'd love to. But what if Diana doesn't like me? It would be the most tragical disappointment of my life."

"I do wish you wouldn't use such big words, Anne. It sounds odd for an 11-year-old to be saying such things. And don't worry, I'm sure Diana will like you just fine."

They walked through the fields to the Barry's house, Orchard Slope. Marilla knocked at the door, and a woman with dark eyes and dark hair opened it. She looked stern and serious.

"Marilla, come in," she said. "And this is the little girl you've taken in, I suppose?"

"Yes, this is Anne," Marilla replied.

"Anne with an 'e'," added Anne.

Mrs Barry led them into the parlour where a girl was sitting reading a book. She had dark hair like her mother but her cheeks were rosy and her eyes sparkled.

"This is my daughter, Diana," Mrs Barry told Anne. "Diana, show Anne the garden. You read far too much and the fresh air will do you good."

Outside, Anne and Diana stood looking at each other shyly. The garden was full of beautiful flowers, old willow trees and tall fir trees. But Anne was too nervous to notice. She so wanted Diana to like her.

"I'm so happy you've come to live at Green Gables," Diana said, with a smile. "It'll be such fun to have someone to play with."

Anne smiled back at her, feeling a little less shy. "And this is a wonderful garden to play in. Do you think your mother would let us build a playhouse over in the trees? I could ask Marilla for some old china and we could make a little table from an old tree stump."

"A playhouse?" Diana cried, clapping her hands together. "What a brilliant idea. I think I'm going to like you, Anne Shirley."

After making plans for their new den, Anne said, "This has been such a fun afternoon. Let's be best friends for ever and ever, Diana."

"Oh, yes!" Diana beamed at Anne with delight. "I've always wanted a best friend."

That evening, Matthew came home from the store with a present for Anne. "I thought you might like these," he said, shyly handing her a small parcel of chocolate sweets.

"Oh, Matthew!" Anne beamed at him. "Thank you."

"Don't eat all of them at once and ruin your teeth," Marilla said, with a sniff. Her brother just couldn't help spoiling Anne.

"I'll just eat one tonight and save half of them for Diana," Anne said. "The other half will taste twice as good if I share them with my best friend."

The trouble with the brooch

Spring turned to summer, and Anne was playing at Diana's house when Diana told her some exciting news: there was going to be a village picnic.

Anne rushed home to talk to Marilla. "There's going to be ice cream, Marilla!" she said, with great excitement. "I've never tasted ice cream. Can I go? Diana says everyone has to bring food for the picnic, but I can't cook. Would you help me?"

"Yes, of course you can go and I'll help you bake."

"Oh, dear, dear Marilla. You're so kind to me."

Anne threw her arms around Marilla and kissed her on the cheek. Marilla's heart leapt. It was the first time a child had kissed her cheek without being told to and Marilla was delighted. Anne was bringing such unexpected joy into their lives.

***

On the evening before the picnic, Marilla came into the kitchen where Anne was helping prepare dinner.

"Anne, have you seen my best brooch?" Marilla asked. "I was wearing it yesterday but I can't seem to find it."

"I tried it on this afternoon," Anne admitted. "I know it was wrong to touch your things, but it's so pretty."

"It's not there now." Marilla sighed. "Did you take it out of the house and lose it?"

"No! I promise. I put it back on your dressing table."

Marilla couldn't help thinking that Anne was lying. What else could have happened to her brooch? It definitely wasn't on the dressing table, and no one else had touched it. She couldn't help feeling deeply disappointed. "Anne, you'll have to go to your room and stay there until you tell the truth. If there's one thing I can't stand, it's being lied to."

"But I'll miss the picnic!" Anne protested, desperate to attend. "I promise I'm not lying."

"I'm sorry, but you can't go anywhere until you confess. That was a special brooch and I'm very upset that it's lost." And Marilla wouldn't be moved on the matter.

Sun shone through Anne's window the next morning; it was the perfect weather for a picnic. She was still upset that Marilla didn't believe her, but she'd come up with a plan.

When Marilla came in with her breakfast on a tray, Anne said, "I'm ready to confess. I pinned your brooch on my dress when I went for a walk near the Lake of Shining Waters. While I was crossing the bridge, I took it off to look at it and it slipped through my fingers. It sank to the bottom of the lake. And that's the best I can do at confessing, Marilla."

"Oh, Anne!" Marilla shook her head. "Why didn't you tell me this yesterday? I'm still very upset. It was my favourite brooch."

"I'm sorry," Anne said. "And I know I'll have to be punished. But can you do it quickly because I'd like to go to the picnic without worrying about it."

"Picnic!" cried Marilla. "You'll go to no picnic today, Anne Shirley. That's your punishment."

"But you promised." Anne clutched Marilla's hand. "That's why I confessed. Think of the ice cream! It's my only chance to taste it. Please, Marilla?"

Marilla pulled her hand away. "You can't, Anne, I'm sorry. You have to learn what's right and wrong. And taking that brooch outside and lying about it was very wrong."

Anne threw herself face down onto her bed and started sobbing. And there she stayed until Marilla came back into her room later that afternoon with a strange expression on her face. "I've something to tell you, Anne. I picked up my black shawl to mend a tear and I found something caught in the lace." She opened her hand. It was the brooch. "Why did you tell me you'd lost the brooch when it wasn't the truth?"

"You said I'd have to stay in my room until I confessed," Anne admitted. "And I didn't want to miss the picnic."

Not for the first time, Marilla wondered if she'd ever understand how to be a parent to an 11-year-old girl.

She stroked Anne's hair. "I'm sorry, I should've believed you at the start and had a harder look for it."

"And I'm sorry for trying on your brooch without asking," Anne said. "I'll never do it again."

Marilla smiled. "Now, get yourself ready for the picnic. You can be there for the ice cream, if you hurry."

"Oh, Marilla!" Anne's eyes sparkled. "Five minutes ago, I was wishing I'd never been born. Now I'm so happy I wouldn't change places with the king himself."

That evening, Anne came back from the picnic with a huge smile. She flopped down on her bed. "Oh, Marilla, I've had the most divine time. Isn't that a wonderfully expressive word? I learnt it today. Words fail me to describe ice cream. It was simply delicious."

The trouble with school

In September, Anne started at Avonlea school where she sat next to her best friend, Diana. For three weeks all went smoothly, but one morning as they walked towards the school building, Diana said, "Gilbert Blythe will be back in school today. He's been staying with his cousins all summer. He's awfully funny, Anne, and he teases all the girls in our class."

When they got to school and sat down in their seats, Diana whispered to Anne, "That's Gilbert sitting right across the aisle from you. Look!"

Anne glanced over at him. He looked at her and winked. Anne turned away quickly. "He's very bold," she whispered back at Diana. "It's bad manners to wink at a strange girl."

Gilbert Blythe hadn't made the best first impression on Anne Shirley.

That afternoon, while Mr Phillips was teaching Maths, Gilbert reached over, held one of Anne's red plaits and said, "Carrots! Carrots!"

Anne was so shocked and upset, she jumped to her feet. "You mean, hateful boy!" she shouted, still as sensitive about her red hair as she'd always been. In a sudden fury, she picked up her book and cracked it over his head. Thwack!

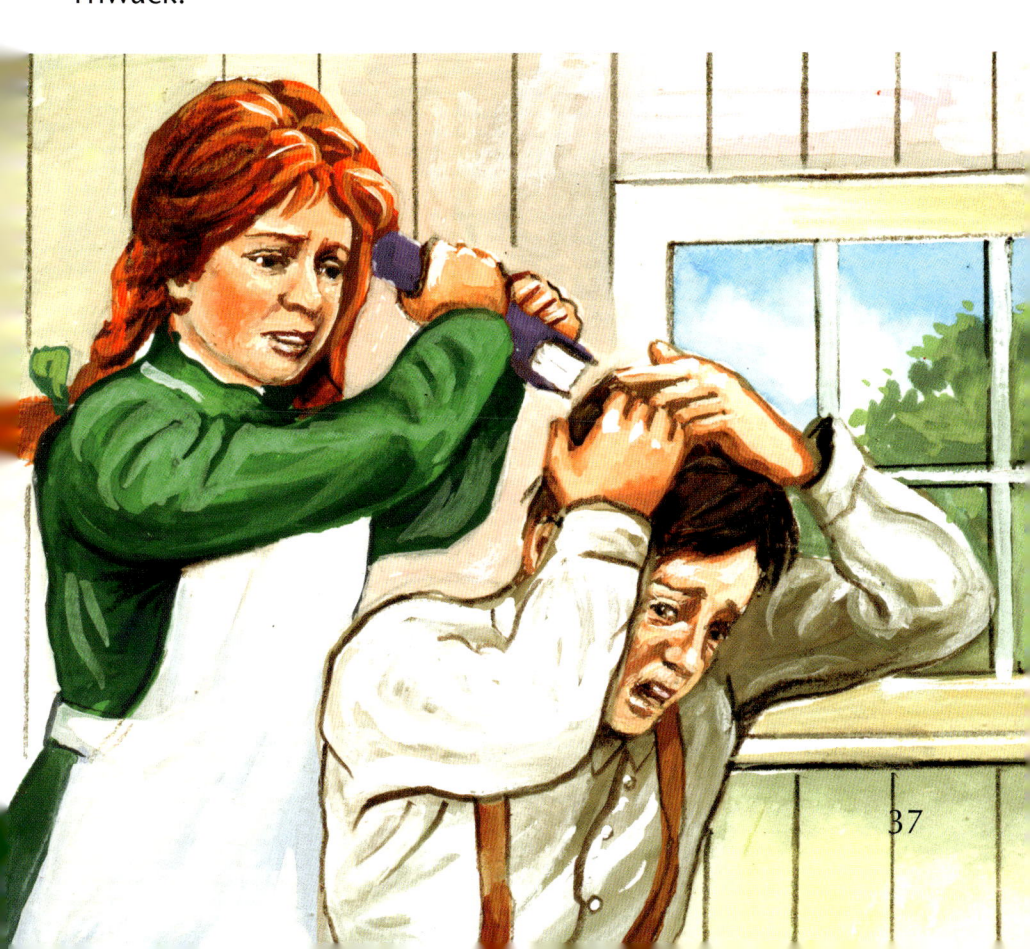

Everyone gasped. Mr Phillips said, "Anne Shirley, why did you do that?"

"It was my fault," Gilbert said quickly. "I was teasing her."

Mr Phillips ignored him. "You must learn to control your temper, Anne. Go and stand in front of the blackboard for the rest of the afternoon." Anne was humiliated beyond despair.

After school, Gilbert was waiting for Anne by the door. "I'm sorry I made fun of your hair," he said. "Don't be angry with me."

Anne walked past him, pretending she couldn't hear. She'd never, ever talk to Gilbert Blythe again. But things were about to get even worse ...

The following day, Anne got in trouble again. Some of the boys as well as Anne were late getting into class after lunch break, but as the last person through the schoolhouse door, Mr Phillips decided to punish only Anne.

"Anne Shirley!" he shouted at her. "Since you seem to be so fond of the boys, you can sit beside Gilbert Blythe for the rest of the term."

As soon as school was over, Anne marched back to her old desk, took everything out and piled it up neatly to take home.

"Why are you clearing out your desk?" Diana asked her.

"I'm not coming back to school," Anne said simply. Being made to sit next to her sworn enemy was just too much for Anne's pride.

When Anne told Marilla what had happened with Mr Phillips and that she was staying at home from now on, Marilla wasn't keen on the idea. "You have to go to school, Anne," she said worriedly.

Anne shook her head stubbornly. "It's not fair, Marilla. The boys were late back to class too and they didn't get punished. I'm not changing my mind and that's that."

"I'm going to talk to Mrs Lynde about all this," Marilla said, with a sigh. "She's put her ten children through school; she'll know what to do."

Marilla came back from Mrs Lynde's with a strange look on her face. "Well, Anne, it seems that Mrs Lynde agrees with you," she said. "She thinks it was most unfair of Mr Phillips to punish you and not the boys. I guess you can stay at home."

Anne smiled. "Thank you, Marilla. I'll miss Diana, but I certainly won't miss that dreadful Gilbert Blythe."

The trouble with Mrs Barry

"Oh, Marilla," Anne said one weekend, "look at the red leaves on those maple trees in the orchard. I'm so glad I live in a world where there are Octobers."

"Indeed," said Marilla. "As I'll be out today, would you like to have Diana over for tea? Matthew will be around if you need anything, of course, but otherwise you'll be in charge."

"Yes! It'll seem so nice and grown-uppish. Can we use the rosebud tea set?"

"No, you can use the brown one. And I'll make you some cookies and one of my special chocolate cakes. Only one slice each, mind. It's very rich."

That afternoon, Diana arrived in her second-best party dress and the girls shook hands gravely, as if they'd never met before. Then Anne showed her guest into the sitting room, where she'd laid out their party tea.

"How is your mother?" Anne asked politely.

"She is very well, thank you. Is Mr Cuthbert keeping well?"

"Why, yes, he is. Thank you for asking."

"And have you picked many of your apples yet?" Diana asked.

"Oh, ever so many," Anne replied, forgetting to be all grown-up and dignified. "Marilla said we could eat any that are left on the trees. And she's made us one of her special chocolate cakes and lemonade."

They sat outside for a while, eating apples. Diana told Anne all the news from school. Then they went back inside and sat down to eat their party tea.

"This cake is delicious," Diana said, crumbs all around her mouth. "The best chocolate cake I've ever tasted. Can I have another slice?"

"Of course," Anne said. "You can have as much as you like. After all those apples, I'm not a bit hungry."

While Diana helped herself to a second and third slice, Anne chattered on happily. "Marilla's such a wonderful cook. She's trying to teach me, but there are so many rules to follow in cookery … " Diana had gone very quiet. "What's the matter, Diana?"

Diana's face was turning very pale. "I don't feel very well," she said. "I need to go home." She stood up quickly and ran out of the door.

"Diana!" Anne called after her. But Diana didn't turn around. What a disappointing end to our tea party, thought Anne as she tidied away the remains of the cake.

The next day, Marilla demanded, "Anne Shirley, what did you do to poor Diana yesterday?"

Anne stared at her in amazement. "Nothing."

"Well, Mrs Barry said you fed Diana so much chocolate cake that she was sick all down her best dress and ruined it. How many slices did you give her?"

"Three," Anne said quietly. "But it wasn't my fault. She liked it so much, Marilla, I just couldn't say no."

Marilla sighed. "I'll go and talk to Mrs Barry. See if I can sort this out."

Marilla came back from Orchard Slope with a face like thunder. "Of all the unreasonable women I've ever met, Mrs Barry is the worst. I told her it was all a mistake, but she wouldn't listen. She said my chocolate cake was far too rich and I'd no business baking it that way. I told her if her daughter wasn't so greedy she wouldn't have made herself sick. I'm sorry, Anne, Mrs Barry says you won't be allowed to play with Diana ever again."

That night, Anne cried herself to sleep again. October was the worst month in the world.

Anne saves Minnie May

Months passed, autumn turned to winter, and Christmas came and went. Anne had returned to school and, although Diana was forbidden to speak to or even look at Anne, at least she could gaze at her old friend and remember what fun they'd had together.

One snowy January evening, Anne was sitting in the kitchen with Matthew when Diana came flying through the door.

"Oh, Diana!" Anne cried, surprised to see her friend at Green Gables. "Has your mother finally said we can be friends again?"

Diana shook her head furiously. "No. But my little sister has a fever and Father and Mother are in town. There's nobody to go for the doctor and our maid doesn't know what to do. Oh, Anne, I'm so scared. Minnie May's only three." With that, Diana started crying.

Matthew reached for his cap and coat. "I'll go and fetch the doctor," he said, before hurrying out of the door.

"Don't cry, Diana," Anne soothed. "Mrs Hammond's babies all had a fever at some point. I know exactly what to do."

The two girls ran through the snow to Diana's house where they found Minnie May lying on the kitchen sofa. She was red-faced and finding it hard to breathe.

49

Anne knelt down beside Minnie May, put her hand on her forehead and then looked up at Diana's tear-stained face. "Minnie May has a fever all right. We need to get her temperature down quickly."

Anne worked tirelessly as evening turned to night. She put soft flannel cloths soaked in cold water on Minnie May's body to cool her skin and gave her sips of water to drink. She never once took her eyes off the little girl.

At three in the morning, Matthew finally arrived with the doctor. By then, Minnie May was over the worst. Her temperature had gone down and she was sleeping.

"Minnie May was so bad, I nearly gave up," Anne told the doctor. "I can't tell you how relieved I was when she started to cool down."

The doctor looked at Anne and shook his head. "You're a remarkable girl," he told her. "You saved that child's life. I've never seen such skill and wisdom in someone your age. Now go and have a good night's sleep. You deserve it."

Anne was so tired, she slept until late in the afternoon. When she finally went downstairs, Marilla looked up from the kitchen table where she was sitting with Matthew and smiled. "Mrs Barry was here earlier, Anne. Minnie May is much better this morning. She wanted to tell you how grateful she is.

"She's sorry about the whole chocolate cake business and says she hopes you'll forgive her. She wants you to be good friends with Diana again. What do you say to that?"

"Oh, Marilla!" Anne sprung to her feet. "I can't wait another minute. I'm going to see Diana right away."

"Wait! You can't go outside without a coat – " But Anne was already tearing out of the door.

Marilla and Matthew watched through the window as she ran towards Diana's house.

"I've grown so fond of that girl," Matthew said. "I can hardly remember life without her."

Marilla nodded. "She's changed our lives, that's for sure. Green Gables wouldn't be the same now without Anne Shirley."

Anne's Avonlea

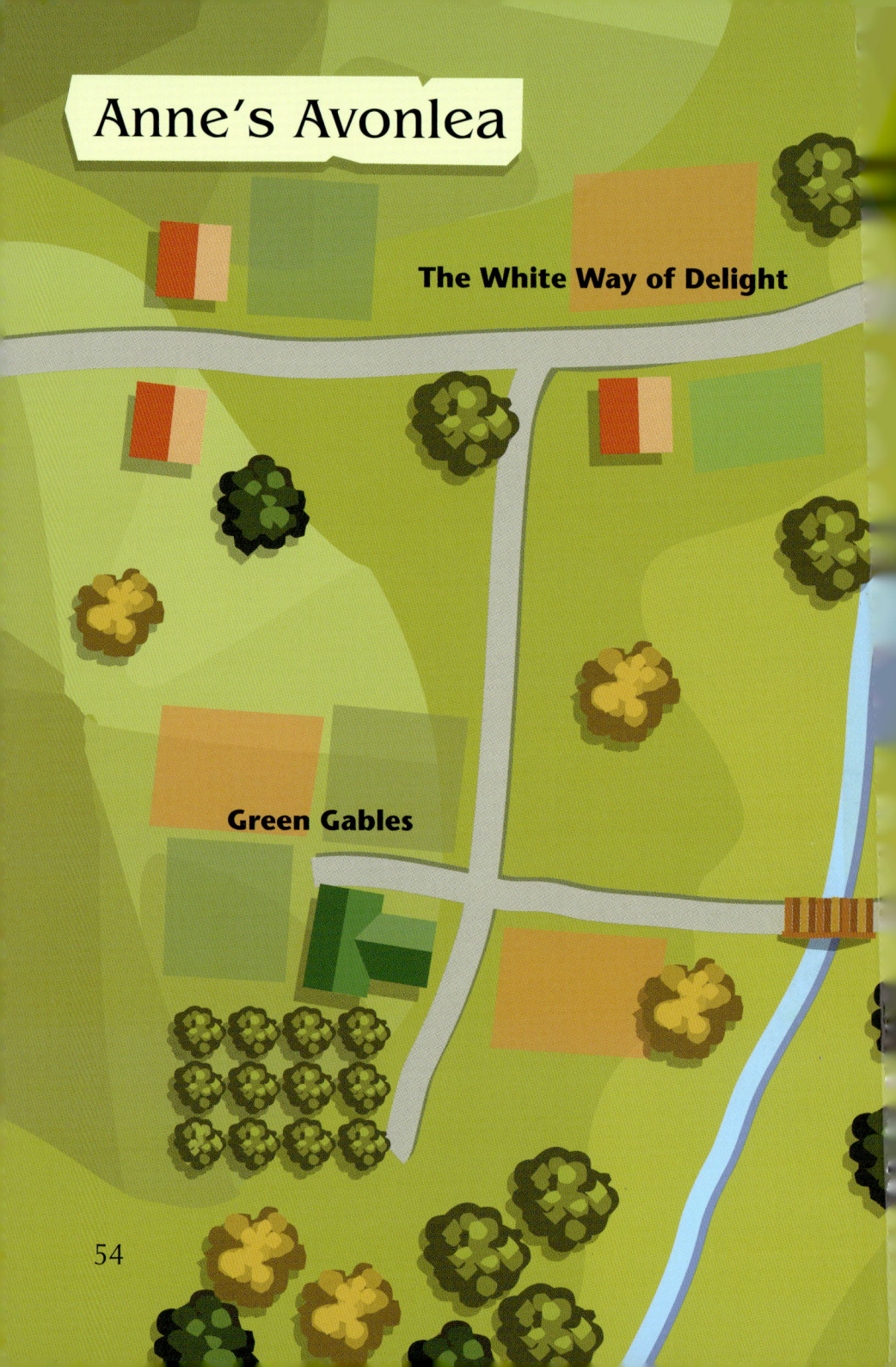

The White Way of Delight

Green Gables

Mrs Lynde's house

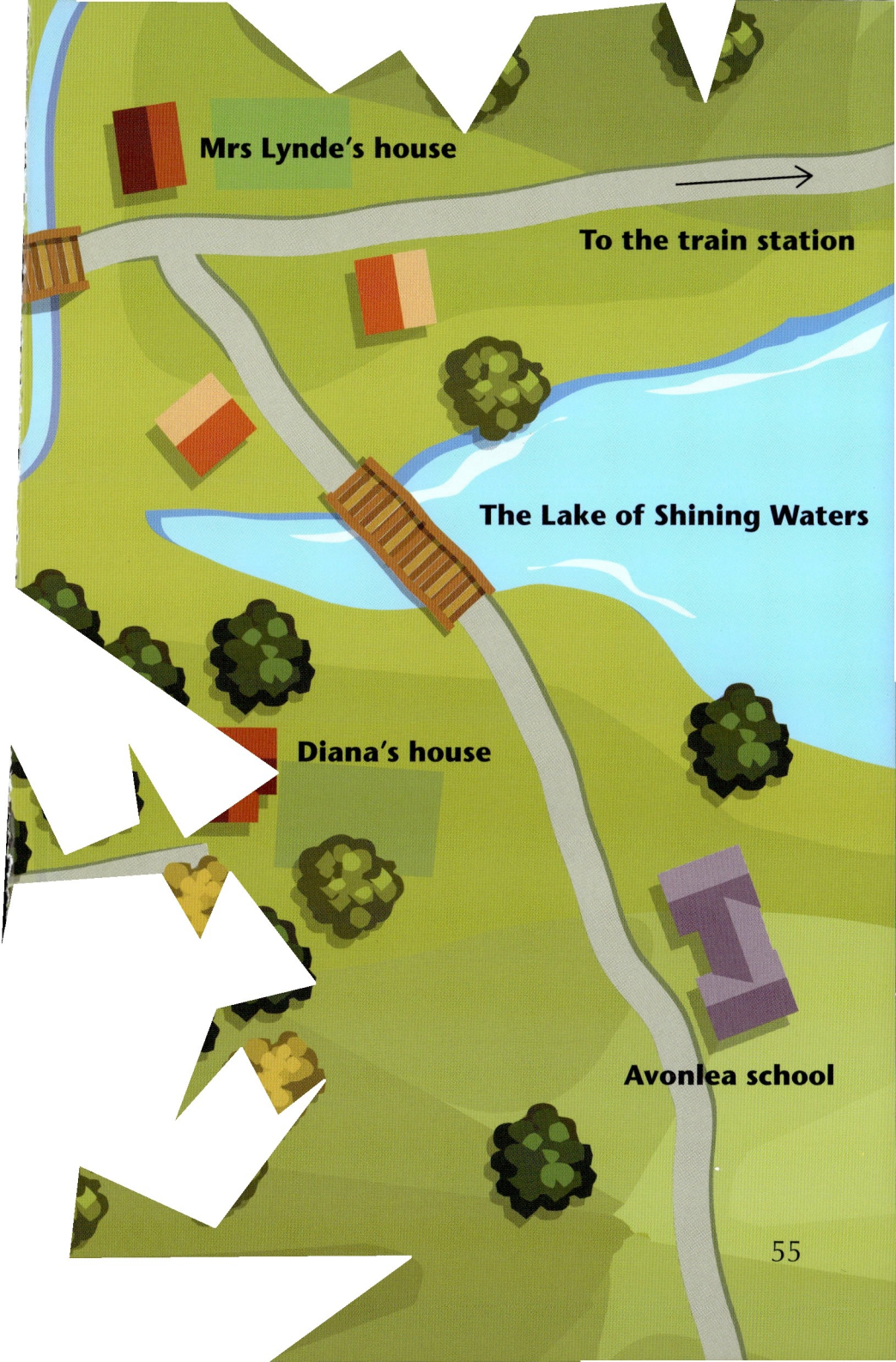

To the train station

The Lake of Shining Waters

Diana's house

Avonlea school

55

Ideas for reading

Written by Clare Dowdall, PhD
Lecturer and Primary Literacy Consultant

Reading objectives:
- identify and discuss themes and conventions in and across a wide range of writing
- ask questions to improve their understanding
- draw inferences such as inferring characters' feelings, thoughts and motives from their actions, and justify inferences with evidence

Spoken language objectives:
- ask relevant questions to extend their understanding and knowledge
- give well-structured descriptions, explanations and narratives for different purposes
- use spoken language to develop understanding through speculating, hypothesising, imagining and exploring ideas
- participate in discussions, presentations, performances, role play, improvisations and debates

Curriculum links: PSHE – relationships

Resources: paper and pencils or ICT for artwork

Build a context for reading

- Look at the front cover and discuss what can be seen in the picture. Ask children to suggest what Green Gables is.
- Explain that this is a classic children's story set in Canada about an orphaned child. Check that children understand what it means to be orphaned.
- Read the blurb aloud. Discuss what is meant by Anne having "a huge impact" on the lives of Marilla and Matthew. Discuss what the title implies about Anne's fate.

Understand and apply reading strategies

- Turn to pp2–3. Ask children to read silently, raising questions about Anne's character to deepen understanding.